Decem

Dear Jessica,

Merry Christmas to
a girl I love!

Love,
Robert

Dogs Have the
STRANGEST
❖ FRIENDS ❖
& Other True Stories of Animal Feelings

Dogs Have the STRANGEST ❖ FRIENDS ❖

& Other True Stories of Animal Feelings

Jeffrey Moussaieff Masson

ILLUSTRATED BY SHIRLEY FELTS

Dutton Children's Books · New York

For Ilan

J.M.M.

To Nick, Martin, and Katy

S.F.

❖ ACKNOWLEDGMENTS ❖

I want to thank Dave Sidon, the director of Wildlife Images in Oregon, and Sheila Siddle, the director of the Chimfunshi Wildlife Orphanage Trust in Zambia, for providing me with material that I used in this book. I also want to thank the wonderful people at Dutton Children's Books: first of all, Donna Brooks, who has a magic hand when it comes to editing; her assistant, Alissa Heyman; copy editors Andrea Mosbacher and Tiffany Yates; proofreaders Shelly Perron and Nora Reichard; and designer Ellen M. Lucaire. I especially want to thank Shirley Felts for her sublime paintings, which I look at over and over, each time with new delight. Finally, I want to thank the children who will read these stories and say, "I always knew that animals had feelings."

Text copyright © 2000 by Jeffrey Moussaieff Masson
Illustrations copyright © 2000 by Shirley Felts
Library of Congress Cataloging-in-Publication Data
Masson, J. Moussaieff (Jeffrey Moussaieff), date
Dogs have the strangest friends: & other true stories of animal feelings/
Jeffrey Moussaieff Masson: illustrated by Shirley Felts. —1st ed.
p. cm.
Includes bibliographical references (p.109). Summary: A collection of true stories demonstrating that animals have feelings, including "An Elephant Saves a Baby Rhino" and "The Sadness of a Peregrine Falcon."
ISBN 0-525-45745-3
1. Emotions in animals—Anecdotes—Juvenile literature. 2. Animal behavior—Anecdotes—Juvenile literature. [1. Emotions in animals. 2. Animals—Habits and behavior.] I. Felts, Shirley, ill. II. Title.
QL785.27.M355 2000 591.5—dc21 99-38945 CIP
Published in the United States 2000 by Dutton Children's Books,
a division of Penguin Putnam Books for Young Readers
345 Hudson Street, New York, New York 10014
http://www.penguinputnam.com/yreaders/index.htm
Designed by Ellen M. Lucaire • Printed in Hong Kong
First Edition
1 3 5 7 9 10 8 6 4 2

❖ CONTENTS ❖

Most of you have probably never had much difficulty recognizing that animals have feelings—strong feelings, much like those you and I have. We feel sad. We feel lonely. We feel happy, even joyful. I believe, and perhaps you may, too, that animals also feel those emotions. Many of you have become close friends with your companion animals (I try to avoid the word *pet*): dogs, cats, birds, or other animals, such as rabbits, horses, hamsters, or gerbils. (I'll bet there is even somebody out there who has become friends with a fish.) Some of you who live on farms may have gotten to know a cow, a goat, or a sheep and have seen them show affection or fear or sadness. Those of you who have lived with animals in your house know that when you call your dog, she comes. Or if you call your cat, he will at least look up to let you know he has heard, even if he decides not to come over to you.

Animals we live with usually know their names, and they know that their names refer to them and only them. They have a sense of identity. When somebody calls out to you on the street, you know that *you* are being called. You have a distinct sense of yourself as a person different from all other people. I believe animals feel this sense of distinctness as well. Moreover, your dog will come to you but usually not to a stranger who calls his name. He knows that *he* is being referred to, but he does not feel close to the stranger, does not trust him yet, and refuses to acknowledge any special bond with him that would cause him to come when called. So the dog is making a kind of judgment as to just *who* is calling. Into that judgment come feelings: the dog feels close or wary, affectionate or indifferent. When *you* call your dog, he runs over, his tail wagging, glad to have been called, and eager to see what you want. When a dog hears your voice among others, he feels happy and shows you his happiness. His wagging his tail is as clear as if he were saying: "I'm glad you called." It is his language, and you understand it perfectly well. Moreover, he *knows* that you know what it means. It is one of the great mysteries and pleasures of life that we understand the physical signs of emotions that dogs use as easily as they seem to understand the signs of *our* emotions.

Even if some of you have never had a companion animal, I am sure you have thought a lot about animals, and it has never occurred to you that a whale or a dolphin or a lion or an ape or an elephant *can't* feel the feelings you imagine them feeling. After all, animals have brains just as we do, and there are parts of their brains that specialize in feelings. In fact, we should always remember that *we* are animals, too. There are many things we share with our animal relatives. We all have developed intelligence that allows us to survive in the environment we are born into. We all have feelings for our families; parents love their children, and children love their parents partly because this helps us to thrive in our world. I believe that just as we have feelings, so do animals. They can feel love and compassion and loneliness and boredom and friendship just as we do. I believe animals have nearly all the feelings we do, and maybe even some that we don't.

Some people are willing to acknowledge that animals *look* as if they feel happiness by the way they move their bodies. But they argue that we can never be certain that the happiness they feel is the same happiness that we humans feel. It is true that when a dog raises her nose and sniffs the air and seems to smile with delight, we may not know exactly what she is feeling. Perhaps the pleasure she takes in the natural world is a little bit different from the pleasure *we* take in that same world. Nevertheless, we recognize what the dog is feeling. So, too, when we see a dog chained up in a yard all by herself, looking lonely and sad, we cannot say that the dog feels exactly what we would feel if confined somewhere. But we know for certain that the dog is feeling *something* like what we feel when we are lonely. We can feel empathy for the dog, just as a dog who has lived with you for years knows when you feel sad and comes over to lick your face or your hand in sympathy. This kind of empathy and sympathy, these feelings that cross over the species barrier and can be felt between two different animals, is one of the great wonders of our world.

Why am I so eager to urge people to see that animals have feelings? It is because for so many years people have been hurting animals, eating them, hunting them, taking their skin or fur for clothing or furniture, performing painful experiments on them, at least in part because they have lost the intuitive appreciation that animals experience suffering and other emotions not so differently from the way we do.

Many indigenous peoples have, for thousands of years, been taking animals' lives for food and shelter and clothing, despite a deep belief in those animals' abilities to feel and to suffer. In fact, *because* indigenous peoples held a deep belief in an animal's soul, in its being, they created and performed rituals to convey their respect for the animal and acknowledge gratitude, even sorrow, for the life they were taking. Today many, perhaps most, people *do* believe that animals can feel things. But this belief is no longer a part of our shared culture and our rituals. Perhaps because of that, we've lost the respect necessary to behave in accord with our belief. Modern urbanized life has removed us more and more from the reality of animal suffering that lies behind much of the food, drugs, and other goods that we enjoy. If our culture could reestablish its understanding that when a cat cries out or a dog shrinks away, it is because it suffers just as we do, then maybe people would be less likely to do the things to animals that cause them suffering.

I am always on the lookout for stories about animal feelings. From time to time, people write to me or call me to tell me their stories. They are true stories, surely, since they come from people who were on the scene, who observed events firsthand. I have enjoyed gathering some of their stories here, putting them together with others of my favorites. I hope you will enjoy them, too.

Dogs Have the STRANGEST ❖ FRIENDS ❖

& Other True Stories of Animal Feelings

CHAPTER ONE

An ELEPHANT Saves a BABY RHINO

t was the rainy season in Tsavo National Park in Kenya, a country in the heart of Africa. All night the rain fell. But early the next morning, the sun shone bright. Delicate white-tailed gnus (grazing antelope), graceful gerenuk (dwarf antelope), quick-running cheetahs, giraffes, zebras, and many other animals had come to a water hole, a pond in a swampy clearing in the forest. Because salt is important in the diets of these wild animals, and because it is difficult to find at certain times of the year, near the water hole the game warden had left out little cones of salt for the animals to lick. At a distance, some people were observing the salt lick. They wanted to see how the animals interacted with one another. Tension is common at a water hole; one animal pushes another out of the way, one takes a swipe at a weaker animal.

What these people were about to see, however, was something wholly different.

A black rhinoceros mother had come to the clearing to eat the soft grasses at the edge of the pond and to lick the salt. She was accompanied by an oxpecker, a little bird that likes to perch on the jaw of the rhinoceros and remove bugs from its skin. Also with her was her young calf, born only a few weeks earlier. Although the people watching did not give the calf a name, we can call her Bicorni, which means two-horned, because she did indeed have two horns, like all black rhinoceroses.

After a while, the mother wandered off a little bit into the forest, looking for tender shoots. It was a hot day, and baby Bicorni waded into the pond water. Rhinoceroses need to spend some time every day in a river or a pond because their large bodies become easily overheated. Bicorni slowly made her way into the water and began playing and rolling around in the soft mud. The mud kept her cool and gave her a thick coating that protected her skin against flies and other stinging insects. But when Bicorni wanted to get out of the pond, the mud sucked at her fat little feet, and she could barely move. As she lifted one foot, the others just sank in deeper. She began to whimper to herself, then called more loudly, her cries sounding like a cross between a calf's squeals and a lamb's bleating. Nobody could mistake the fact that she was frightened and wanted help.

The mother rhinoceros came out of the forest and ran up to her baby. She sniffed her skin and pushed her with her head, hoping to free her. But Bicorni was stuck. The mother stood for a moment, as if thinking. Then she butted her head against Bicorni's stomach; but this, too, failed to help. The mother turned and walked back to the edge of the forest, where Bicorni could no longer see her. Now the little one began to bleat more loudly than ever.

At that moment a herd of elephants arrived at the salt lick. They were all female, because once young male elephants reach ten or eleven or twelve, they leave their herd and go off on their own. Only the females—sisters, aunts, cousins—stay on together. Elephants, like rhinoceroses, need a great deal of water. In fact, they require nineteen to twenty-four gallons of liquid every day. So the whole herd marched down to the pond to drink and cool off.

At the head of the herd was the oldest elephant, the matriarch. Since elephants grow all their lives, she was also the largest. Adult elephants are so big and strong that they have no natural enemies except humans. Lions have been known to attack elephants, however. And black rhinoceroses, which are territorial and quick to become angry, will charge any animals that encroach on their territory, including elephants. Usually, however, their meetings at salt licks and watering holes are peaceful. (Once some elephants were observed teasing a baby rhino by kicking dust in its face—there are bullies in every playground.)

Bicorni was frightened and tired. She called out again. This time it was not her mother who responded, but the matriarch. (Let's call her Cyclotia, since the scientific name of the forest elephant is *Loxodonta cyclotis*.) Cyclotia was enormous, with long, strong ivory tusks. Though she had poor vision like all elephants, she did have a wonderful tool for investigating the world around her: her trunk. A trunk is an elephant's nose, but it can do much more than smell. With her trunk, Cyclotia could eat grass from the ground or pull leaves from high branches. If need be, she could wrap her powerful trunk around a tree and rip the whole thing right out of the earth. When Cyclotia crossed a river, she simply walked along the bottom, her trunk held high in the air like a little periscope, allowing her to breathe. At the tip of her trunk she had fingerlike lips so delicate that she could pick up a twig no larger than a safety pin. To show affection to her offspring, she would hold the tip of her calf's trunk and blow warm air into it.

Cyclotia now ran her trunk all over Bicorni. Elephants caress one another with their trunks in greeting, so this may have been her way of introducing herself to Bicorni. But in doing so, she may also have been checking to see what was wrong. Evidently she correctly understood the problem. Of course, she could see, smell, and hear that Bicorni was no elephant cub, but a member of a different animal group. This did not seem to affect her actions. She knelt down, put her long, strong tusks underneath the baby rhino, and began to lift.

At the edge of the forest, the mother rhino watched warily. Even though elephants eat only plants and are generally peace-loving, the mother rhino must have been nervous seeing such a large, powerful animal kneel next to her helpless calf. Not taking any chances, she came charging toward Cyclotia.

Now elephants, in spite of their huge bodies, are nimble and quick—an elephant can run twenty-five miles an hour, faster than any human. As the rhino charged, Cyclotia merely stepped aside and ambled off to join the other elephants quietly licking salt and enjoying themselves in a different part of the pond. She didn't seem bothered by the attack. For her part, the mother rhino went back to the forest.

But Bicorni was still stuck and still calling for help. Again Cyclotia came to the calf, knelt down, and began to lift her out of the mud with those long, strong tusks. And again the mother rhino came charging out from the edge of the forest. Four times the elephant matriarch came back to try to free the baby rhino. Four times the mother rhino charged. Finally Cyclotia gave up and moved off with her herd, leaving Bicorni to her fate.

The people who had been watching were astonished that an elephant would try to help the rhino. After all, elephants and rhinos are members of different species, and scientists

have long believed that an animal will help only a member of its own species, especially if giving help is in any way risky. But no doubt many wonderful things happen in the jungle that no human is around to see. That nobody sees them does not mean they do not happen.

This time, however, humans were present, and they wanted to help Bicorni, too. The next morning, they found the baby rhino still stuck, so they began to approach her. As they came near, Bicorni began to bellow. Knowing that Bicorni's mother would return at the sound of her cries, the humans quickly moved away. Looking back, they saw that Bicorni had at last managed to pull herself free. She ran joyously off to her mother, and together they strolled off into the forest. Maybe that mother rhino had known all along that her young calf would be able to manage all by herself! Maybe that was why she walked off into the forest, seemingly unconcerned. To the human observers, Cyclotia, the compassionate mother elephant, was a heroine. She had definitely shown compassion to a member of another species.

And I wouldn't be surprised if Bicorni never forgets that kindness. Perhaps she herself will do some gentle deed for another animal in need when she grows up.

CHAPTER TWO

A MOTHER ELEPHANT Saves Her BABY from a FLOOD

n 1920, Lt. Col. J. H. Williams went to Burma, as the country was then known. (It is now called Myanmar.) Nestled between India, Pakistan, and China in the north, Laos and Thailand in the east, and Bangladesh in the west, this Southeast Asian country is rich in hardwood forests. Williams went to Burma to work for the Bombay Burma Trading Corporation, a company specializing in exporting this valuable timber.

His job was to supervise the seventy elephants employed hauling teak trees at jungle camps on the Upper Chindwin River. The Upper Chindwin winds through the monsoon forests in the northern hills region of what was formerly

Upper Burma. In these hills lived animals like the Himala-yan black bear, the huge flying fox (actually a bat), dangerous wild buffalo, and the small barking deer known as *gyi*. No machinery could penetrate the thick forests where the teak trees grew. But elephants could. And elephants were strong enough to move the heavy timber to the nearby rivers that would float it downstream to Mandalay or the capital, Ran-goon, nearly a thousand miles away. The trunk of a teak tree could take up to one year to reach its destination.

Some of the working elephants had been brought from India, a few from Thailand, but most of them had been cap-tured wild in Burma and broken in. Although these elephants had been tamed, they were not really domesticated the way a dog or a cat or even a horse is domesticated. Elephants rarely give birth except in the wild. They are wary of humans, and we are wary of them. You could not walk up to a strange ele-phant and pet him the way you could a dog.

The elephants who worked the timber farms in up-country Burma hauled trees for only part of the twenty-four hours in the day. They worked in the early morning when it was cool. In the afternoon, their hauling gear removed, they were allowed to go into the jungle to find their own food and water. Each elephant had an "Oozie" (the Burmese word for *mahout, driver, keeper*) who rode on the elephant's neck and was his best friend. Today in the forests of Myanmar, elephants still haul hardwood timber and still have Oozies. Often an Oozie and his elephant grow up together, remaining inseparable until death. It is the Oozie's job to get up in the morning well before dawn and track his elephant through the jungle. He might have to travel as far as eight miles before he finds her. Each elephant wears a bell that the Oozie has hollowed out from a lump of teak, and it wears hobbles that keep it from moving too fast and too far in the wild.

When an Oozie spots his elephant, he sits down and slowly calls the elephant: *"Lah! Lah!"* ("Come on! Come on!") After a while he will change the words: *"Digo Lah! Digo Lah!"* ("Come here! Come here!") When the elephant finally comes, the Oozie talks to her slowly and soothingly for several minutes. Then comes the command: *"Hmit!"* ("Sit!") The elephant drops on her haunches and extends all four of her legs. The Oozie removes the cane hobbles and climbs onto her head. *"Tah!"* ("Stand up!") he tells her, and off they go, back to the elephant camp.

Once in the camp the Oozie washes his elephant in the river and then harnesses her for work. Generally the work begins with climbing a ridge two thousand feet above the camp. There the elephant grasps a huge tree trunk, perhaps twenty feet long, and drags it for a mile along the top of the ridge. This can be dangerous work. The elephant and Oozie practice great skill and teamwork. When they reach their destination, the elephant puts the log down near the edge. Then she may tease her Oozie. She may push the log right to the edge of the cliff but wait a bit while her Oozie gets more and more annoyed. Finally she gives the log the extra little shove that sends it crashing four hundred feet down the cliff to the water below. Then she will turn to the Oozie with a look of great satisfaction, as if to say, "That was nothing, mere child's play."

Colonel Williams—or Elephant Bill, as he became known throughout Burma—was a great lover of elephants. He thought them the most intelligent of all animals. The elephant "never stops learning," he said, "because he is always thinking. Not even a really good sheepdog can compare with an elephant in intelligence." To prove his point he told the following story.

One evening during the monsoon season, the Upper Chindwin River was flooding, becoming powerful enough to carry logs down. Elephant Bill was listening, hoping to hear the boom and roar of timber coming from upstream. His camp was perched atop steep, rocky riverbanks, twelve to fifteen feet high. The banks on the other side of the river, fifty yards away, were ledges of hard mud. Although it was dusk, Elephant Bill could see these ledges being submerged one after the other as the river flooded and the water quickly rose.

He was suddenly alarmed to hear an elephant roaring as though frightened. Looking across, he saw three or four men rushing up and down on the opposite side of the river in a state of great excitement. Realizing that something must be wrong, he ran down to his edge of the riverbank to see if he could help. There he saw Ma Shwe (Miss Gold), one of the prize working elephants, trapped with her three-month-old calf in the fast-rising torrent. Ma Shwe could still stand, as she was more than seven feet tall and the water was not yet over six feet. But a life-and-death struggle was taking place between her calf and the churning river. The calf was screaming in terror and floating on the river like a cork. Ma Shwe was as close to the riverbank as she could get, turning her whole body against the raging river and letting the torrent press her calf against her massive body. Every now and then the swirling water would sweep the calf away; then, with terrific strength, Ma Shwe would reach out, encircle her baby with her trunk, and pull the calf upstream to rest against her body again.

Suddenly the water rose as if a large wave had come down the river. The calf was washed clean over her mother's back and carried away. Ma Shwe turned to chase her. She traveled about fifty yards downstream, now plunging, now floating, finally crossing to the other side of the river before she could catch up with her baby. For what seemed like minutes she pinned the calf against the rocky bank. Then, making a gigantic effort, she encircled the calf with her trunk, reared on her hind legs, and placed the calf on a narrow shelf of rock five feet above the flood level.

The effort was too great for her. Ma Shwe fell back, and the raging torrent swept her away. Now she would have to fight to save her own life. Less than three hundred yards downriver was a steep waterfall. If she were carried over the

falls, it would mean her certain death. One spot between her and the waterfall finally afforded her some footing. But it was on the side opposite her calf.

Elephant Bill peered over at the baby from about eight feet above, wondering what he could do to help. The calf stood tucked up, shivering and terrified, on a shelf of rock just wide enough for its feet. Its fat little belly protruded against the ledge. Then, "I heard the grandest sounds of a mother's love I can remember," Elephant Bill wrote. "Ma Shwe had crossed the river and got up the bank and was making her way back as fast as she could, calling the whole time—a defiant roar, but to her calf it was music. The two little ears, like little maps of India, were cocked forward listening to the only sounds that mattered, the call of her mother."

The colonel saw Ma Shwe emerge from the jungle and appear on the opposite bank. When she spotted her calf she stopped roaring and began rumbling, a sound not unlike that made by a very high-powered car when accelerating. It is an elephant's sound of pleasure, like a cat's purring. It showed the delight she must have felt to see her calf still in the spot where she had placed her half an hour before.

As darkness fell, the muffled boom of floating logs came from upstream. A torrential rain was falling, and the river still separated the mother and her calf. Before turning in for the night, Elephant Bill twice went down to the bank and shone his torch on the calf. But it seemed only to disturb her, causing her to flap her ears in warning, so he went away.

At dawn, Elephant Bill arose, wondering what he would find. The swollen river had subsided to a mere foot of dirt-colored water. He looked across, and there, on the far bank, were both Ma Shwe and her calf. Somehow Ma Shwe must have lifted her calf down and walked her across the river to the other side. No one in the camp had seen her recover her calf, but she probably lowered her from the ledge the same way she had lifted her up there.

Five years later, when the calf came to be named, the Burmese christened it Ma Yay Yee (Miss Laughing Water).

The love that Ma Shwe showed for her calf is in no way unusual among elephants. Elephant mothers seem to love their babies as much as human mothers love theirs. But it is unusual for humans to be able to witness such love so directly. That is what makes this story important as well as touching. It shows us, once again, that we are not alone in our love for children. Many animals share this with us.

CHAPTER THREE

The MOTHER CAT Who Went into the FIRE to Save Her KITTENS

ivonia Avenue is a pretty tough street in a part of Brooklyn called East New York. There are lots of pit bulls and Rottweilers on that street, so it is not exactly a safe street for cats. During one of the roughest winters in recent history, in the middle of a snowstorm, a year-and-a-half-old stray cat was pregnant, looking for a place to have her kittens. She found it in an old abandoned garage. Homeless people were living there, and the cat found the most comfortable spot she could in a quiet corner of the large deserted building. That is where this cat, later named Scarlett (after Scarlett O'Hara in *Gone With the*

Wind), decided to have her kittens. She had five of them: a white, a dark gray, a black and white, a Siamese, and a smoky gray. For a few weeks, everything seemed to go well for the young mother and her litter of five.

Then, just before dawn on Friday, March 29, 1997, when only Scarlett and her kittens were in the garage, it seems somebody started a fire there on purpose. It was a raging fire, with a thick black column of smoke rising into the sky. Neighbors had gathered around by the time the fire trucks arrived. One fireman, David Giannelli, a softhearted animal lover, heard faint meows and followed the sound to the brick building next door. He discovered three kittens huddled against a wall, mewing and crying, perhaps in shock. He found a box for them and gave it to a neighbor to put in a safe spot. As the fire came under control, David heard more faint crying and soon located two more kittens across the street. He realized that the places where he had found the kittens formed a kind of straight line—as though a mother cat had carried each kitten out of the burning building, deposited it safely away from the fire, and then gone back into the flames to retrieve the next. The fireman knew that cats usually try to hide from fires, and then bolt when that becomes impossible. So this must have been one brave mother cat. But where was she now? With some other firemen he searched, and in a vacant lot across the street, behind a pile of rubble, he found her.

He scooped her up and put her in the box with her kit-

tens. Despite the burns on their ears and paws, and the singed patches on their fur, the kittens began to mew, happy to have their mother back. Scarlett pressed her nose against each one as though silently counting to make sure they were all there and to let them know she was with them. Then she dropped down, exhausted but purring loudly. Her kittens had been saved.

It seemed to observers that while the kittens were safe, the mother was not. The five laps in and out of the smoke and flames had taken a terrible toll. Her blistered eyes were swollen shut. Her mouth, ears, and face were scorched. Her mammary glands had been badly burned, and so had her ears and the pads of her feet. Her coat was singed away in some places. And who knew the state of her lungs? Still, she was alive, even if in terrible pain.

The firemen rushed the mother cat and her kittens to the North Shore Animal League, where a team of veterinarian doctors, led by Dr. Bonnie Brown and Dr. Larry Cohen, were called to operate on the brave little mama. The doctors were afraid that the burns would become infected, and that she would lose her sight. They were not even sure she would live. But she was a fighter, and live she did, as did all but one of her kittens. A few days later, as news of the mama cat's valiant rescue spread throughout the world, six thousand people wrote letters asking to adopt her and the kittens. (Now Scarlett and her kittens are all members of caring households.) Even Oprah Winfrey said on her show in 1997: "Look at us! Not a dry eye in the house! We're crying over this cat!" So did I. Who wouldn't be moved by this story of one cat's extraordinary act of courageous love?

CHAPTER FOUR

A GORILLA Saves a YOUNG BOY

onkeys and apes (also called the great apes) are very different animals, even though they are both primates (mammals, of the same family that includes humans). Monkeys are small, with tails. There are hundreds of different kinds. But there are only four great apes, which are large primates with no tails. Three of the great apes live in Africa: gorillas, chimpanzees, and bonobos (also called pygmy chimpanzees, even though they are about the same height as other chimpanzees). The fourth great ape, the orangutan, is from Sumatra and Borneo.

The gorilla is the largest of the great apes. The highly endangered mountain gorillas live in moss-shrouded forests at altitudes of more than ten thousand feet along the Virunga range of volcanoes on the Rwanda-Zaire-Uganda border. Only about 450 of them survive in the wild. The Eastern Lowland gorilla is the largest gorilla. The dominant male, called a silverback (because of the conspicuous silvery-gray saddle on his back) can weigh up to five hundred pounds and grow to be well over six feet tall. Between four and eight thousand Eastern Lowland gorillas survive in isolated patches of rainforest in Zaire. The Western Lowland gorilla is the smallest (but males are still three hundred pounds) and most populous, with about forty thousand in the forests of Cameroon and other African countries. Depending on its size, a gorilla has the strength of perhaps half a dozen men. With its powerful jaws and large formidable canine teeth, a gorilla (though vegetarian) can be a dangerous animal, even when caged in a zoo. Gorillas (and other animals) have different "rules" for behavior than human beings do. What works in a gorilla community may not work when you put a frail "human" into the mix.

August 16, 1996, was a hot Friday at the Brookfield Zoo near Chicago. The exhibit that everybody wanted to see was the famous Tropical World, featuring seven Western Lowland gorillas. One gorilla, the popular eight-year-old female Binti-Jua, carried her seventeen-month-old daughter, Koola, with her wherever she went. Binti-Jua was considered a very good mother.

Her own childhood had not been easy. She was born in the Columbus Zoo in Ohio on March 17, 1988. Binti-Jua's mother was herself raised in captivity and did not know how to be a mother. Normally a young female gorilla watches her own mother over the years and learns from observation how to be a nurturing female, much as human females do. Binti's mother treated her daughter with indifference. So humans had to cradle Binti and hand-feed her with a bottle every two hours. As she grew, other female gorillas groomed her and got her used to their company. Because Binti-Jua was reared in part by humans, her keepers were afraid she would not know how to be a mother herself. So they taught her how by using dolls. She learned very quickly and well. Once, when she was living at the Children's Zoo in San Francisco, a toddler walked up to her, face-to-face. Binti behaved beautifully, reaching out gently to touch the little child.

On that Friday in 1996, a little three-year-old boy and his mother were visiting the zoo. The boy was so eager to see the gorillas that, as they got closer to the Tropical World exhibit, he ran on ahead. When he reached the gorilla enclosure, he immediately climbed the barrier to get a better view of the gorilla area twenty-four feet below him. As his mother hurried up to him, the boy suddenly lost his balance and plunged down into the enclosure. He landed on his bottom on the concrete. From where visitors were watching, it looked as if he were unconscious, perhaps even dead. People ran away from the exhibit screaming for help.

Before any of the zookeepers could reach the enclosure, Binti, her baby on her back, rushed over to the boy and gen-

tly picked him up in her arms. The other gorillas started to come over, too, but Binti walked away from them. Cradling the boy, she headed to the enclosure entrance, forty feet away. She knew that was where the zookeepers would appear. Sure enough, when she arrived, the zookeepers were already there, waiting for her. Binti carefully put the boy down and backed away. The zookeepers entered and carried the boy out.

While all this was taking place, somebody with a video camera recorded the episode. Once everyone realized that the gorilla had rescued the boy, a kind of hush went through the crowd, and then cheers. Within hours the story was in the news around the world. Nobody before had witnessed such an act of compassion on the part of a great ape toward a human.

The little boy was rushed to Loyola University Medical Center in nearby Maywood. At first he was listed in critical condition; the staff at the hospital did not know if he would live or die. But in a few days he made a good recovery and now is completely well, with no injuries at all—except to his memory: he cannot remember falling into the pit and being rescued by Binti-Jua. Maybe it will all come back to him in a dream someday. And maybe he will grow up to become a great scholar of the primates, like Jane Goodall.

CHAPTER FIVE

The GRIZZLY BEAR and the CAT

ave Sidon is the director of an animal rehabil-
itation center called Wildlife Images in Grants
Pass, Oregon, near that state's border with California. Everybody for hundreds of miles around the center
knows that if they find an animal in trouble—a bird with a
broken wing, a baby bobcat wandering in the road—this is
where they can bring it. Dave has the reputation for never
turning anyone away. He has loved and cared for wild animals in trouble ever since he was a little boy. He was one of
the lucky people who got to turn his childhood passion into
a job for the rest of his life!

About ten years ago, a little bear cub had been looking

for food on the railroad tracks in Montana when he was hit by a train. The cub received terrible head injuries, and when he was brought to Wildlife Images nobody expected him to live very long. But Griz, as he came to be called, made a remarkable recovery. Still, even though he grew into a physically healthy adult bear, something seemed to be lacking: there was no apparent aggression in him. Dave was afraid that if he let Griz go in the wild, the bear would refuse to hunt and might starve to death. So the center kept him in a special large enclosure all by himself. He had many toys to play with. Some of the staff thought he might be lonely and wished they could find him a mate. But they were afraid that with his unusually gentle nature, he might not be able to stand up for himself. So they kept him alone.

One warm day in July, something strange happened. A tiny six-week-old orange kitten, weighing less than a pound, had been abandoned near the center. She was terrified of humans and would not let anybody near her, not even to feed her—and she was very hungry. Griz was eating his midday meal—a five-gallon bucket of kibble, meat, fruits, vegetables, and venison. The kitten wandered over to the bars of the enclosure and watched. She then squeezed her scrawny little body through the bars and walked over to the six-hundred-pound bear. Dave Sidon happened to be on hand at the time and saw what was happening. Now, gentle as Griz was, Dave still fully expected the cat to become a snack for the bear.

(Bears are omnivores; that is, like humans, they eat just about anything. They mostly live on honey and berries, but they will also eat the young of moose, beaver, deer, anything they feel like eating.)

Dave got an enormous surprise: Griz looked over at the starving runt of a kitten and looked back at his food. He then pulled out a piece of chicken with his paw and gently dropped it. The kitten crept forward, hesitating. Then she ran right up and ate the piece of chicken in one big gulp. The bear took out some more meat and put it down next to his paw. Again the kitten ate. Dave turned to a friend who had hurried over. "I have never seen anything like this before," he said. The great big grizzly bear was feeding a minuscule kitten as if she were a bear cub.

Each time the kitten downed a piece of meat, the bear would put another piece next to his paw. The kitten was making up for lost time and could barely stop. Finally she was satisfied and, with a big yawn, lay down next to the bear and fell asleep.

The next day Dave found the kitten in the same spot. And when it was time for the bear's meal, Griz took out a little bit for the kitten—that day, and the next day, and the next. Soon they were the best of friends. All day the six-hundred-pound bear and the small kitten, who was quickly growing into a cat, would play together. The cat would lie in ambush for Griz, then leap out and swat him on his nose.

Griz would let her ride on his back, and when he carried her around, he carried her in his mouth! There are people who say that all of this happened because the bear was brain damaged. Maybe. But maybe, just maybe, that bear recognized a friend when he saw one, and that kitten knew she had found a home.

❖ CHAPTER SIX ❖

DOGS Have the STRANGEST FRIENDS

It may be that dogs have a greater ability to make friends than humans do. Dogs are friends most of all with other dogs, then with humans, and then sometimes with cats. Daniel Pinkwater, in *The Soul of a Dog*, writes about a dog, Arnold, taking care of an eight-week-old kitten. Arnold wanted nothing more than to go to sleep in his private corner. But every time the kitten cried, he'd drag himself to his feet and slouch over to the kitten's cage. There he would lie down with his nose between the cage wires and let the kitten knead him with its tiny claws. When the kitten became quiet, Arnold would head for his corner and flop down, exhausted. As soon as the kitten started to cry again, Arnold would haul himself back to the cage.

One of the most unusual dog friendships on record involves a lion. Rick Glassey, who for twenty years has been training exotic cats for films such as *The Jungle Book*, received a call one day from Lauri Marker. She worked in the Winston Wildlife Park in Oregon, and she had a favor to ask. Because she was leaving for Africa to continue her study of cheetahs, would Rick be willing to take care of one of her animals?

"Sure, no problem," said Rick. "What have you got?"

"Just a dog. A Rhodesian Ridgeback, a female, about a year and a half old."

Rick liked dogs and was willing to help. Rhodesian Ridgebacks come from South Africa, where they were once bred to hunt lions. Large, brave dogs, wonderful with people, they are fearsome in the field.

"One other thing," added Lauri. "The dog comes with her best and only friend, a lion called Wazoo."

It seems that Wazoo, the lion, was housed from the day he was born with a family of dogs: a Rhodesian Ridgeback mother and her four puppies. Because the puppies' father was probably a Border collie, the puppies were smaller than normal Rhodesian Ridgebacks. And they were only a few months older than the lion. The puppies and the lion had grown up together as brothers and sisters. One puppy in particular seemed closer to the lion than to her own littermates. She had developed into a handsome bitch, weighing about fifty pounds. This was the dog Lauri wanted Rick to take, along with the lion. The lion was also handsome, but he was enormous, weighing more than five hundred pounds.

When Janee (an African word meaning both *yes* and *no*), the female Rhodesian Ridgeback, and Wazoo, the lion, arrived at Rick's, he took them to a preserve in Soledad Canyon, California, just north of Los Angeles. Shambala Preserve was founded and is now directed by Tippi Hedren, an actress who has dedicated her life to helping lions, tigers, leopards, and other big cats who have not been able to find homes. There the dog and the lion lived in a one-acre compound with a river running through it.

Wazoo and Janee were inseparable friends. The lion would spend hours licking the dog's ears and face. When he finished, she would begin grooming him all over his enormous body. At night they would sleep together in a tight ball, each holding on to the other. "How could this unlikely bonding have come about?" I asked Rick. He explained that in the beginning it wasn't only out of pure love that they stayed together and remained close. No doubt the lion loved the dog and the dog loved the lion, but something else was at work here—at least in the opinion of one of the world's foremost trainers of wild cats.

Rhodesian Ridgebacks are famous for their ability to bluff. Lions come from tight-knit social groups, the lion pride, consisting of between four and twelve related adult females, their offspring, and from one to six adult males. In the pride,

hierarchy plays an important role. Every animal needs to know where he or she stands in rank, and it is rare that any attempt is made to break out of that rank. Rick felt that somehow Janee had convinced the lion that she was his superior, that she was dominant over him. During the early years of their friendship, the lion accepted this. The dog was his boss, no question about it.

The smallish dog, though physically far inferior to the five hundred pounds of solid muscle that was her best friend, nonetheless had a toughness that allowed her to insist on being deferred to by the larger animal. Janee demanded respect, and she got it. Wazoo was very good-natured and rarely did anything to offend the dog. If he did, Janee quickly brought him around: she would attack him with fierce barking, snarling, growling, and even occasional bites to the ear. The lion would slink away, apologetic for having annoyed his friend and master.

For seven years the two animals romped and played and got intense pleasure from each other's company. Is it possible that the dog believed she was a small lion, and the lion believed he was a large dog? Or were they simply not aware of any species barrier? They would eat together, though if push came to shove, Janee got the lion's share. When they were young they would split a baby bottle of milk, each licking from it at the same time. If the dog had to leave the large, fenced area for any reason, the lion would begin to pace up and down, clearly anxious. He found the separation uncomfortable. There was no doubt that Wazoo missed Janee. When his friend returned, he would greet her as if she had been gone for years, running up to her and licking her from head to toe, maybe to examine her and make sure nothing bad had befallen her. Janee would wag her tail in ecstasy, equally happy to be back with her close companion.

After seven years, Rick noticed over the space of a single week that Wazoo was undergoing a change. He could see something dawning in the lion's eyes. Wazoo seemed slowly to be coming awake. It was like watching somebody emerge from a long sleep, as if the lion were saying to himself, "Wait a minute, I'm not a dog; I'm a lion, and that small animal over there, she's no lion—she's a mere dog." One day, when Janee started to punish the lion for some minor thing he had done, the lion's eyes grew dark with anger. Wazoo turned and uttered a deep growl—unmistakably a threat, and one dangerous to ignore. The dog was puzzled, but when she tried to force her dominance, the lion would take it no more. Wazoo ran at the dog, and Janee, realizing the game was up, turned around and raced for the water. Fortunately Rick was there in time to remove the shaking dog from the compound. Had she remained another hour, Rick told me, the lion would have undoubtedly killed her. Rick never dared put them together again.

What happened? What broke the bond? How could it be that these two lived like intimate friends for seven years, and then it all just ended? It is impossible to say what was going

on in the lion's mind. The dog's fear was obvious, the lion's awakening more obscure.

Wazoo still lives by himself at the Shambala Preserve, sleeping peacefully, as lions will, most of the day. Janee lives with Rick's father-in-law in Ukiah, in northern California, a dog who loves being a dog now and is best friends with her human companion.

I wonder if either animal is ever nostalgic. Does the dog think back with longing for the days when her closest friend was a lion? Does the lion ever wonder why he spoiled a beautiful friendship with a dog?

SOMETIMES DOGS MAKE FRIENDS with much smaller animals. Janis, who teaches English at St. Mary's College in Moraga, a town in northern California not far from Berkeley, tells the following story.

She was once watching her dog, a giant Newfoundland named Oliver, running and tumbling in the grass in her backyard. He seemed to be happily playing with a toy. The toy, it turned out, was a small brown bunny. Janis was sure the rabbit was about to turn into the dog's supper, but to her astonishment it proved not so. The dog would chase the rabbit around in a couple of tight circles, and then the rabbit would dash off—only to double back, close enough so that the dog would begin running after her again.

The rabbit had been a pet—that much was clear, given

her friendly behavior. Perhaps she had escaped or been let go. In any case, she was now living like a wild rabbit. One day Janis saw the rabbit attempting to involve the sleeping dog in a chase. Oliver lifted his head and opened one eye but didn't seem interested. The rabbit knew how to get his attention. She ran directly at him, leaped straight up at the last moment, spun in the air, and landed a blow with both back feet square on his nose. The chase was on. At the end of the chase, both animals went to sleep, the rabbit nestling on top of the enormous Newfoundland. That rabbit knew she was no dog; she just wanted to play. Often the big dog would sleep on the back porch at night, the small rabbit curled against his stomach. The friendship lasted for two years. Then, one day, the rabbit just disappeared as mysteriously as she had arrived. Let's hope she found some other bunnies to play with as happily as she romped with Oliver.

HORSES AND DOGS OFTEN become quite friendly with one another. Dogs will even make friends with burros. Jim, a sculptor and iron forger from Sonoma, in northern California, told me about working on a ranch outside Phoenix, Arizona. He had a dog, an Australian shepherd by the name of Jellybean. Jellybean grew up with a burro named Nicholas. When the burro was a baby and Jellybean was a pup, they became inseparable friends. The burro would call out early in the morning, a noise that sounded like an old car

horn honking. The dog would race over to the pasture where the burro slept, jump the fence, and join his friend for their first walk of the day. As they became adults, they remained close, lying next to each other in the pastures and running together in the hills. During the day, as a special sign of affection, the burro would suck the dog's ears (this is how burros show their love). When night fell, the dog would jump up on the burro's back, and the two would go to sleep under the quiet, star-studded desert sky. Jim says that he can never forget looking out his window at dusk and hearing the burro calling his friend Jellybean to come spend the night. The dog would race over, leap onto the back of the standing burro, and settle in for the long sleep ahead.

Do you know any unusual friendships between dogs and other animals? I'll bet you do.

CHAPTER SEVEN

How to Make
FRIENDS with a FLY

I cannot guarantee that the following story is true. I read about it in a book, and it startled me. The author said it was true. Here is the reason I was amazed.

Many of us think we love animals. Some of us can carry that love pretty far. We take animals to doctors when they are sick; we sleep in the same room with them; we celebrate their birthdays; we buy them toys and games. I do not like the thought of eating my friends, so a while ago I stopped eating animal flesh. I do not even like the thought of hurting my friends, so I try not to eat anything that comes from an animal if it involves harm: I will not eat eggs unless I know that they were laid by chickens who are free to live outdoors and who will not be killed when they are too old to lay any more eggs. I stopped drinking milk because I believe that a cow or a goat produces milk for her own babies, not for us. And I gave up butter and cheese, too. (It is not always easy for me, especially forgoing cheese, which I love. Milk was easy to give up because wonderful-tasting substitutes, soy milk and rice milk, are so easy to buy now. Of course, many vegetarians do use dairy products; I may be a little extreme here.)

I try not to kill any animal. I used to kill ants when they invaded my kitchen, but not anymore. Now I try to talk with them—of course, in a language they can understand. And since ants seem to like sweet things, I talk honey. I find out where the ants enter my kitchen; then I put a little pot of honey in that spot. In a few days all the ants have left the kitchen and are eating the honey out of the jar. It really works well, for both sides. They get their food and I get a kitchen free of ants, except for one small spot, which is kind of fun to look at because I get to watch all the little creatures pouring in and out of the honey pot all day, taking little trea-sure balls of honey back to their hill homes. It sure beats squashing them by the thousands.

There are only two kinds of insects that I kill: mosquitoes and fleas. Mosquitoes because they attack me. Fleas because they attack my dogs and cats. Perhaps some people will think I am being inconsistent, but those are my reasons. I used to kill flies. But when I tried to come up with a reason,

I would say, "Well, just because they're flies." Flies posed a problem, you see. I had no real reason to kill a fly—I just didn't like them buzzing around me and landing on my food. They looked so dirty. But are they really so dirty, or do they even look dirty up close? Had I ever looked at a fly carefully? Were they really my enemy?

I have to admit that I had not thought all that much about flies, and what they are like, until I read an account of a man who made friends with a fly. I was amazed. The man was J. Allen Boone, and he wrote a little book with a big idea in the title, *Kinship with All Life*. He wrote it a long time ago, in 1954. Everybody who reads this book is immediately converted into an animal lover! In this book, Boone says that one day he was shaving in the bathroom when an ordinary fly (you will see that he was not so ordinary in a minute) flew into the room. The fly followed Boone into the kitchen and sat and watched him as he ate. When Boone began to write, the little creature sat on top of his paper. When he got up, the fly followed him, like a tiny, buzzing airplane. Boone was enchanted. He put his finger out and invited the fly to come aboard. The fly did a little hop, and presto, he was up on his finger. There he began studiously to wash himself, using his two little front legs carefully to groom each of his other four. Then he stopped and looked at his new friend the writer with what seemed like curiosity. Boone tossed him into the air, and the fly circled slowly above his head. And when Boone pointed his finger up, down came the little guy, land-

ing on the fingertip. Boone reached over and began slowly stroking the insect's wings. The fly seemed to like it.

The next day, who was waiting in the bathroom? Freddie the Fly—Boone had now given the fly a name. The fly quickly hopped up onto the writer's finger, to get stroked. After a little while, the fly flew off. But the next day when the man came into the house, he saw that very same fly come straight in the window and without hesitation land on his outstretched finger. Boone could now walk around the house, with the fly perched there, attentively watching everything that was going on. The fly had become tame! Now first thing in the morning, the fly would be waiting for him and would immediately fly over to him and land on his finger. Boone wondered where Freddie the Fly went at night, but he could never discover the answer. In the morning, bright and early, Freddie would be waiting for him on the mirror in the bathroom.

Was Freddie a very special fly, or is it possible that all flies have in them the capacity for friendship? Humankind has believed for centuries that flies are simply nuisances at best, spreaders of disease at worst, to be killed on sight. Hardly the stuff of friendship. Could everybody be wrong about this? Is Boone perhaps the first human to recognize that a fly can feel?

It is hard for us to imagine the emotions of a fly—those slight buzzing creatures are so different from us. But all of us know that flies land on us—and then appear afraid, for they fly away from us when we move fingers in their direction. The fact that this fly did not suggests that he might have felt something different was going on with Mr. Boone. The fly, I venture to say, *trusted* him. And, because the fly did this every day, we might even say that the fly liked being with the man, that it seemed to give the fly pleasure to be with him. The fly may well have been as curious about the man as the man was about him. Certainly he was curious about something, or he would not have allowed the man to carry him around the house so freely. So, odd as it may sound, because a fly seems capable of some sort of trusting relationship with a person, maybe we could allow ourselves to wonder if perhaps flies can feel fear, and trust, and pleasure, and curiosity?

How far can we go? Mr. Boone said that he considered the fly a friend, and even that he felt love for the fly. He did not want to hurt it, nor did he want anybody else to hurt that little fly. I can believe this man. But why is it so much harder for me, for us, to believe it possible that the fly felt something like love for the man? That the fly, too, was capable of feeling something like friendship for the man? Perhaps it would not be the exact same feeling in the man and the fly, but something that could somehow be recognized across the great gulf that exists between flies and people.

Have you ever noticed how hard it is to kill a fly with your hand? They are very fast. But every once in a while, I have been able to kill one. I always thought that it was because that particular fly was slow and I was just very fast that day. But now I have a terrible thought: what if that fly was trying to make friends with me and hoped that I would pick it up, not expecting me to kill it?

Maybe the reason we have seen so little friendship between humans and flies is that we have so rarely ever even tried to become friends with a fly. I know I never tried before. Maybe we should. But be careful whom you tell. They might think you are crazy—or anyway that you have been reading some pretty weird books!

CHAPTER EIGHT

How Stupid Can a MAN Be? The ELEPHANT and ME

This is a story about what happened to me before I knew anything at all about elephants. In fact, what I knew about elephants, or rather what I thought I knew, was all wrong, because I had learned about elephants from reading *Babar* and from going to the circus. You cannot know what the real animal is like from that!

One day in 1988 I was visiting south India with a friend and two children. We were staying on an island that is a game preserve. Early in the morning we left the teenagers asleep and walked several miles deep into the forest. Suddenly we saw a herd of wild elephants peacefully grazing. My friend stopped at a respectful distance and began to take some pictures.

I said to her, "Why stop so far away? Come on, let us introduce ourselves to them."

She thought I was crazy to think I could walk right up to a herd of wild elephants and talk to them. She was right, but I did not know it. "Jeff, these are not circus animals; these are not tame elephants. They are wild, and you cannot get too close."

"Nonsense," I said, refusing to listen, "just watch."

I approached to within a few feet of the largest elephant I have ever seen. She looked like a house compared to the small baby next to her. I clapped my hands to get her attention, and then I began chanting in the language of ancient India, Sanskrit, thinking she would recognize this as a holy language and be friendly with me. I even had the fantasy that perhaps she would bend down and let me ride her through the forest! That's how ignorant I was.

Well, she lifted her head up, saw me standing a few feet from her baby, and flapped her ears. I turned to my friend, as if to say, "See, she is waving hello." But an elephant, I now know, waves her ears in anger, not in greeting. A second later the enormous animal trumpeted so loudly that it made my whole body shake. Then she charged.

I could not believe this was happening to me. It was like a moment from a very bad, frightening dream. I turned and ran, screaming, "Help! Help! An elephant is after me!"

But there was nobody to hear me except my friend, and she had hidden her eyes in her hands, afraid of what she was

about to see. I ran wildly to a tree, thinking that perhaps I could climb it and be safe. But the branch I tried to reach was too tall, and I failed. It turned out I was lucky, for later I was told by an elephant expert that had I climbed the tree, the elephant could easily have plucked me down like a ripe plum and stepped on me. I ran blindly through the tall grass, stumbled, and fell to the ground. I looked up to see the elephant stop and use her trunk to try to smell me out. Elephants have poor eyesight, and she had lost sight of me. She turned back to the tree, the last place she had seen me, and ran at it.

I got up very quietly and tiptoed my way back to where my friend was. I was safe, barely. My ignorance had almost cost me my life. When we returned to our hostel, I told the manager that he should put up a sign: WILD ELEPHANTS: DO NOT APPROACH.

He said that was not necessary: "You see, sir, most people already know that they should not walk up to wild elephants!"

He was right. How ignorant can one be? I tried to make up for it in later years, and that is how I came to read about the true behavior of wild animals. I did not want any more fantasies. They were too dangerous!

CHAPTER NINE

The PARROT Who Says He's SORRY (and Means It, Maybe)

I am sure that you have heard the expression "to parrot." It means to repeat what somebody is saying without understanding it. We use this phrase because for centuries people have known that parrots can repeat human *sounds* but have believed that parrots do not know what those sounds mean. When a parrot says, "Give me a cracker," the parrot does not know what a cracker is, right? Wrong! We have recently learned that parrots, at least some of them, know perfectly well the difference between a cracker and a slice of bread. When they ask for one, they want that, not the other. Furthermore, some parrots, when asked the name of something, can tell you the answer.

One parrot already knows the names of fifty objects. If

you point to a set of keys, he will tell you they are keys. And if you then point to a ball, he will tell you it is a ball. Moreover, if you ask him what shape the ball is, he will tell you it is round. If you ask him if the key is round, he will tell you it is not. And when you ask him what color the ball is, he can tell you: red, if it is red, or blue, if it is blue. He knows seven different colors. He can also tell you how many balls there are on the table—so long as there are no more than six. If there are seven, then the parrot cannot answer, because he cannot count beyond six. You can also show him two balls and ask him which one is smaller. He will answer correctly.

Who is this genius parrot? His name is Alex, and he is an African gray parrot trained by psychologist Irene Pepperberg, a scientist who is interested in learning about the intelligence of birds. But Alex is not really a genius. If he were, his achievement would not be so interesting to us. He is just an ordinary parrot, and presumably any African gray parrot could learn to do what Alex does. Several others already have.

The special method that Dr. Pepperberg uses to teach Alex is called rival-model reward training. It works like this: Dr. Pepperberg trains Alex in the presence of a rival, or a model; in this case a human graduate student, who learns alongside Alex. Dr. Pepperberg shows the student a green apple and asks what color it is. Sometimes the student responds correctly, saying *green*. Dr. Pepperberg praises her to the sky: "Yes, yes, Gail. Very, very good. You are a wonderful student, a good student, I am so happy that you got that right." And then, most important of all, she gives Gail a reward, something that parrots love, like a piece of banana or apple.

Alex watches all this with great interest. When Gail makes a mistake and calls the green apple red, she gets no praise and no reward. Alex, fascinated, catches on to the system, and he wants to be the one to get the praise (which parrots love) as well as the food reward. So he learns to answer correctly. He is not just memorizing, because the objects change all the time. He has to learn their names. And he has. When he is shown an unfamiliar object and is asked its color, he answers correctly. And before Gail, too! Alex *knows* the color of the apple and he knows that when he says the correct color, he will get what he wants.

Alex is only a parrot, and parrots cannot be expected to work all day. He gets bored easily, and when he is bored, he becomes naughty. Sometimes he gets angry and does something bad, like grabbing Dr. Pepperberg's pencil and breaking it into little pieces just when she is writing down some important piece of information. Dr. Pepperberg tells him "No! Bad boy!" much as one would do with a dog, and then she walks out of the room. Parrots are very social creatures, like wolves, dogs, and humans. In the wild, they live in large flocks and interact with one another constantly. When they are born in captivity or are caught and put in a cage, they hate to be left alone. If there is no other parrot to become

friends with, then a parrot will become close to the person he lives with.

To bring Dr. Pepperberg back, Alex has learned a very special phrase, one that many people find difficult to say: "I'm sorry." When he says it, she comes back into the room, and their games or the learning continues. Does Alex know what to be "sorry" means? Probably not, in the sense that he does not know the meaning of each individual word: *I* and *am* and *sorry*. Maybe he does not feel guilt, only frustration. But he knows that when he says "I'm sorry," he gets results. His friend returns. And so he uses it.

One day he did something that astonished Dr. Pepperberg and made her wonder if she truly appreciated just how much Alex understood. He was very sick and needed to go to the vet for lung surgery. When the vet asked Dr. Pepperberg to leave the surgery room, she turned to go. Suddenly Alex called out, "Come here. I love you. I'm sorry. I want to go back." Evidently, he thought he had done something bad, and that to punish him she was leaving. But what is amazing is that somehow he connected being sorry with love and staying together. Mighty sophisticated for a little parrot. And these phrases, whatever he thought them to mean, carried a great deal of emotion for Alex. We know this because he was using the language of feelings, and using that language correctly and effectively to hold on to the emotional closeness he clearly desired.

CHAPTER TEN

An ELEPHANT Is Adopted

he following story cannot be doubted, because the whole event was filmed by Derek and Beverly Joubert for their documentary *Reflections on Elephants* for the National Geographic Society. It took place in Africa, in Tsavo National Park in Kenya, with Mount Kilimanjaro visible just across the Tanzanian border. Snaking through the park of almost two and a half million acres is the Galana River, with its seasonal spring-fed swamps. One hot afternoon in Mzima Springs, a lush oasis where black hippos breed and enormous baobab trees provide nesting sites for many parrots (the park is host to four hundred different species of birds), many animals were resting in whatever shade they could find. The oasis is on the edge of a savanna woodland, so lions, giraffes, gazelles, and reddish brown waterbucks (a kind of large, shaggy antelope) were there. Gerenuks (tall, deerlike animals with long necks and legs and narrow heads), the lesser kudu (a large African antelope that can easily leap eight feet), and elephants had also come to cool off and drink. All of these animals usually keep to their own group, because that is where they feel safest and most protected.

In the evening, around dusk, when the animals headed back into the forest, a very young elephant calf had no group to follow, nowhere to go. Perhaps he had become separated from his herd. Or, for reasons we cannot know, perhaps he had been abandoned by his mother. Now he was on his own and all alone. He began to call out piteously.

Elephants, when they are young, are a little bit like babies; although they can walk, they are clumsy, often tripping over their own trunks. Much like humans, they are dependent on their mothers for many years, until they are adolescents. So for this baby to be all alone at such a young age—well, there was just no hope that he would survive.

The tiny elephant calf began pacing in the shallows of the watering hole, wailing and calling out in the night, clearly hoping his mother would hear and come to get him. Making such a racket was a dangerous thing to do, but the calf was too young to understand how important it was for him to be silent on the savanna. If you are small and vulnerable and all alone, the last thing you want to do is attract your enemies' attention. Sure enough, a group of hyenas hunting nearby heard his pitiful wails and started trotting toward the water hole. Without a herd to protect him, the tiny elephant calf would make an easy victim.

At that moment, however, a herd of elephants appeared on the horizon and came charging and splashing into the water. The hyenas retreated, recognizing that they were out-matched. Maybe the elephants thought this lone calf was one of theirs and had mistakenly become separated from them as they left the water hole. They examined the baby by sniffing him. By using their sense of smell, vision, and good memories, it soon became clear to the elephants that this lit-tle calf did not belong to their herd. Probably they under-stood that he had been abandoned. Maybe they even knew why. (Possibly he was born very small or in some other way ill-equipped to survive. It is also possible that his mother had been hunted and that he had escaped. This, too, is informa-tion the elephant herd may have garnered.) In any event, without taking the calf, the elephants left the watering hole.

As soon as the elephants departed, the hyenas returned. They formed a circle around the baby, making the satisfied grunts that indicated a meal was on its way. The poor calf screamed in terror. Nearer and nearer they came, their teeth bared, salivating in preparation for the kill.

Maybe, as they were leaving, the elephants had begun to realize that the hyenas would inevitably return. Or maybe they responded to the hyenas and the screaming. Or maybe they just had second thoughts about leaving that pitiful little elephant to his doom at nightfall. Whatever the reason, as the hyenas were closing in, the group of elephants came charging back. Those hyenas could not get out of there fast enough! The little calf, squealing with delight, dashed right into the middle of the elephant herd and hid among their massive legs. It was almost as if he were pleading: "Please let me stay; I'm all by myself and very frightened."

The elephants seemed to appreciate the danger. Surely they knew that the tiny elephant could not survive on his own. This time they accepted the baby elephant into their ranks. As the herd slowly left the watering hole, the little fellow was smack in the middle, right behind the biggest female. Within minutes several other females came up to examine him. He was now a member of their group, and these "aunts" would nurse him and guide him as he grew up. They had adopted him, with all the obligations this implies in elephant society: years and years of protecting, feeding, and teaching him the ways of elephants.

There is a mystery as to how the elephants came to do "the right thing" with this baby. Did one elephant, the oldest female, make the decision to adopt him and the others go along? Or did the group choose? Was it made without any sounds passing among the animals? Or was there "discussion"? Elephants often "speak" using sounds too low for the human ear to pick up.

Wildlife researchers have not known elephant herds un-

der ordinary circumstances to adopt abandoned calves. In this case, however, the herd did, and we are fortunate enough to possess a film of it. It teaches us once again how little we really know about this most noble of all animals, the elephant. In some ways, elephant mothers are more like us than any other animal. They love their own children as deeply as we love ours—and even, sometimes, the lost children of other elephants.

CHAPTER ELEVEN

A HIPPO Breathes Life into a GAZELLE

nce again, nobody can ever doubt that the following story really happened, because some years ago, purely by chance, the whole remarkable event was captured on film. It occurred at a watering hole in Kruger National Park. Covering almost five million acres in what is called the lowveld in South Africa, Kruger National Park is one of the world's oldest and largest animal preserves. It lies along the Mozambique border, stretching from Zimbabwe south almost to Swaziland. In the park are to be found 480 species of birds, along with elephants, leopards, giraffes, black rhinos, lions, and warthogs. There are the more exotic antelope, among them sassabies, built for speed and endurance, and the shy sitatunga, which by day hides in rivers and lakes and comes ashore at night. This is true of its cousin the nyala as well. Then there are the gregarious and oxlike elands (they can weigh up to two thousand pounds and jump six and a half feet in the air). They have nearly straight horns and fearless ways—females defend the young cooperatively, even advancing together against lions. Finally you could see the greater kudu, very tall and narrow-bodied, with small heads and huge, cupped ears.

One day, near a river and watering hole, a female impala (a species of antelope) was guarding a group of newborn calves. The rest of the herd of females and small calves was feeding nearby on the rich grasses that line the banks of the rivers in the park. One little calf with a long neck, her black-tipped ears twitching, had wandered away from the group. She was eating by herself on the grassland. She was too young to know how dangerous it was to have left the group. Or maybe she did not realize that she was on her own, so intent was she on nibbling the tender shoots.

It was a still day; all was quiet. Suddenly the sensitive ears of the adult impalas picked up danger, and the whole herd was alert—all but the little calf. From the edge of the woodland, a pack of African hunting dogs (also called Cape hunting dogs), lean, lank animals with hyena-like heads, black faces, and tan foreheads, ran into the clearing next to the watering hole.

All animals fear the African hunting dog. Large packs have been known to bring down zebras and even the giant elands routinely. Now the young of all the animals ran toward their parents or toward their group.

The little impala had strayed too far to get back to her herd. Cut off, she began calling out in panic. But it was too late. Nothing could help her now—except her own swiftness. She began to run as fast as she could—to run for her life. The wild dogs were right behind her. When she reached the river, there was nowhere to go but in. So in she leaped.

At that moment, a seven-foot-long, gray-olive Nile crocodile raised his head above the water. With his long jaws and prominent teeth, he was a terrifying sight, weighing at least two thousand pounds. These ferocious animals will ambush antelope, buffalo, zebras, and people. The dogs stopped on the bank. Realizing that a greater predator had appeared, they turned and left. The crocodile swam swiftly over to the impala, grabbed her in his enormous jaws, and dove under the water to drown the little calf. She struggled desperately but seemingly in vain.

Nearby was a large group of hippopotamuses. Nocturnal animals, they spend the hot day resting in the water. At night they wander several miles from their water source to graze before returning in the early morning to their water refuge. Hippos are enormous animals, second only to elephants in size, easily weighing four thousand pounds. They are also dangerous animals: they have bad tempers and huge teeth and can cause death to humans.

Suddenly one female hippo noticed the crocodile with

the impala in his jaws and moved away from the group in his direction.

Crocodiles and hippos are not enemies; they rarely interact with each other at all. Very much unlike the flesh-eating crocodile, hippos are vegetarian, eating only plants. Hippos and crocodiles therefore do not compete for the same food. So that is not the explanation for this hippo suddenly charging the crocodile. Hippos are territorial, however, so perhaps the crocodile had "crossed the line," and that is why she charged. In any case, charge him she did.

The crocodile quickly let go of the impala, swam some distance away, and then stopped—as if to see what the hippo could possibly want with a baby impala. Was the hippo threatening the crocodile for reasons that had nothing to do with the impala—but with territory, perhaps? If that was the case, the crocodile could wait and go back for its prey.

The hippo began gently pushing the wounded impala toward the river's edge. Once there, the hippo used her giant muzzle to help the impala climb onto the steep bank. The impala limped away; then, seriously wounded by the crocodile (or perhaps just in shock), she collapsed on the grass.

The hippo climbed out of the river and walked over to the small impala lying on the ground. She opened her enormous jaws and breathed warm, moist air on the impala. Apparently vivified by her newfound protector, the impala struggled to her feet and tried to walk. After only a few steps she collapsed again. Clearly she was gravely hurt. The hippo approached and again breathed life and courage into her. Again the impala got up and tried to walk but fell to the ground. Five times in all the hippo persisted in trying to use her own breath to revive the small calf. It was not to be. The crocodile had mortally wounded her. Sadly, the fifth time the impala could no longer rise, in spite of all the efforts the hippo had made. She lay back down and died. The hippo left, and the crocodile climbed the bank to claim his prey.

Animal experts, viewing this footage, have struggled to understand what was happening. Nothing like this had ever been seen before, but here it was, captured in black and white on film. What could possibly explain the kindness this hippo showed the little impala? The hippo would seem to have had nothing to gain from trying to help. In fact, she was taking a risk by attacking the crocodile, for this ferocious animal might well have fought back, inflicting injury on the hippo. In all likelihood, the hippo and the impala did not know each other before. They are from two distinct animal groups. We can only guess why this particular hippo showed what looks to us like unusual kindness and concern. My guess is that the hippo was touched by the suffering of the impala and wanted to help. She behaved with what we call compassion.

People who study hippos say they have never before seen a hippo do anything like this. They go on to say that compassion from one wild species to another is something recorded rarely, if at all. But never seen does not mean never happens. After all, why should humans be the only species able to feel compassion for other creatures, ones not like us? Maybe many animals do, and there is just no filmmaker around in the forest to record it.

Whatever the explanation, the hippo deserves our special praise and respect. I cannot help wondering if she went on to rescue other animals.

CHAPTER TWELVE

The SADNESS of a PEREGRINE FALCON

ave you ever seen a falcon? It is a kind of hawk. In fact, its other name is duck hawk, on account of the waterbirds that were this falcon's traditional prey. With its hooked beak, long claws (called talons), and sharp, bright eyes, it looks something like an eagle. Falcons are raptors; that is, they eat other animals, primarily other birds and rodents. Peregrines that now nest and live in cities often eat pigeons. Sometimes falcons fly low to the ground, snatching their prey as they fly. They can also seize other birds in flight, striking them with "fisted" (their claws balled up to form a fist) feet in special "power dives" they use for the occasion. During these power dives, falcons can fly up to two hundred miles per hour, as fast as the fastest sports car. Imagine a sports car coming out of the sky at you! That sense of overwhelming, deadly descending speed is probably what a falcon's prey momentarily experiences.

It is common to see falcons, males and females, perform swift, spectacular, noisy aerobatics over the places where they nest. Some of these aerobatics are part of courtship. But later, at other times, are the falcons just happy to have families, or do these antics mean something else? If they can feel happy, is it also possible that they can feel sad? Can any bird feel sad? Many scientists doubt it, claiming that an animal as little developed (in terms of complexity of brain and nervous system) as a bird cannot possibly feel a deep emotion. (Think of the silly term we often use—and should not: *birdbrain*.)

One respected scientist changed her mind on the matter of birds and feelings, based on something she observed in Colorado. This is her story.

Peregrine falcons tend to nest on ledges high in the mountains. Some falcons in Ethiopia build their nests—their aeries—in the cliff hollows at the very top of a mountain fifteen thousand feet high. In the Rocky Mountains, biologist Dr. Marcy Cottrell Houle was observing the aerie of two peregrine falcons. She had named them Arthur and Jenny, and probably they were, like many falcons, mated for life. Five small baby birds, or eyases, inside the nest kept the male peregrine very busy going out and back finding food for them and his mate. For about the first two weeks of their lives, the eyases' downy feathers were not long enough to keep them warm, so the female peregrine stayed on the nest to brood them. After that, both parents did the work of finding food for their fast-growing young.

Hidden in the bushes, Marcy observed these birds for many hours each day over a period of weeks. One day she noticed that Jenny, the mother, did not leave or return to the nest at all. Only Arthur came and went. That was strange. Where could Jenny be? Also, Arthur seemed different—not his usual self. Normally when he arrived with food, he took it straight into the nest and immediately flew away to seek more. Now he just stood outside the nest for an hour or more. Marcy had never seen him do that before. What could it mean?

Marcy also noticed that when Arthur arrived at the nest now with the food, he would call out for his mate. After calling, he would cock his head and wait, listening. He would call again and again, but no answer came. When there was no reply, he looked into the nest and uttered a sound: "Echup," perhaps his language for "Are you there?" The only answer was silence. He left in evident distress, without feeding the babies.

For three days Arthur, who must have been sleeping elsewhere, would come to the nest, call, and wait in vain. Then on the third day, perched by the aerie, Arthur did something that Marcy had never observed before. He uttered an unfamiliar sound, more like a human moan, the cry of a creature who was suffering. It seemed as if Arthur had finally realized that Jenny was not coming back to the nest. Dr. Marcy Houle heard the sadness in Arthur's cry and wrote: "I will never doubt that an animal can suffer emotions that we humans think belong to our species alone." Most likely Jenny had been shot.

Dr. Houle continued to watch the nest to see what would happen. After Arthur uttered the strange cry of sadness, he sat motionless on the rock and did not move for a whole day. He did not feed himself, and he did not feed his babies. There could be no doubt that he missed Jenny and did not know what to do without her. In a human, we would call this kind of sadness depression. Finally, on the fifth day after Jenny disappeared, Arthur seemed to come out of his depression. Perhaps he realized that his babies were starving. He went out hunting; for the whole day he would come back to the nest, feed the eyases, and rush out again to find more food. He did not stop to rest even for a minute. He was doing the work of two, for normally falcons share this task. Never had the researcher seen a falcon work so hard.

But the days when he was depressed and unable to take care of his five babies had taken their toll: three of the eyases starved to death. Still, two of them were doing fine under their father's care and grew up to be strong birds. One day they took off from their nest to find their own mates and aeries where they could raise their own families. Probably they now knew what hunger meant and would never allow their children to go hungry. Or so I like to think.

CHAPTER THIRTEEN

ELEPHANT BONS

ecause elephant bones are often found heaped together in one spot, some people once believed that elephants went to special elephant graveyards to die. This is probably not true. Most likely the idea resulted from hunting practices that involved killing several elephants in the same place and at the same time. But what probably is true, according to Cynthia Moss, a researcher who has studied wild African elephants for years, is that elephants think about death. They seem to realize that their lives can come to an end. This is why, I believe, they are strongly interested in elephant bones, though not the bones of other animals.

When elephants come across bones from other elephants, they examine them, running their trunks over them, smelling and turning them over, touching them everywhere. They even will pick bones up and sometimes carry them for quite a distance. Skulls and tusks seem to interest elephants the most.

Moss suggests that the elephants may be trying to identify the individual to whom the bones belonged. I wonder whether they are interested in the tusks because they are trying to figure something else out. I think they are trying to figure out why humans kill elephants for their tusks. I think it makes them angry. Some elephants have seen humans kill members of their herd. Some baby elephants have had the horrendous experience of seeing their mothers killed in front of their eyes. I am sure they cannot understand why humans would harm an elephant simply to get its tusks. Of what use to a human is an elephant's tusk? Humans are not elephants and do not need such gigantic teeth. Wildlife researchers know that sometimes elephants will remove a tusk from a dead elephant and hide it in the forest. Is it not possible that they want to make certain no humans find it?

Elephants seem to have a kind of ceremony around death —a death ritual, perhaps. When an elephant dies, the herd will circle the dead companion, shuffling slowly, their heads and trunks hanging down. It is as if they are hoping that by walking around the dead elephant, they can make her stand up again. After a while, when she does not move, they stop circling. Now each elephant faces outward in the circle. This is the reason it seems like a ritual. Otherwise why wouldn't the elephants face in different directions? But they only face out, as if they were performing a kind of ceremony. (Or perhaps they find the sight of the dead animal too painful to look upon without interruption.) Their trunks hang limply down. Then they turn toward the dead elephant and prod her, as if they cannot really believe she is dead. They circle again, and again come to a halt facing outward. Finally, perhaps realizing the elephant is truly dead, they tear out branches and clumps of dirt and grass and put them on her, almost as if they wanted to bury her. (Elephants will sometimes toss grass and dirt onto young calves who are overcome with heat prostration to cool them off. So perhaps this "burial" is somehow associated with that.)

Moss tells of once bringing into her camp the jawbone of a dead female member of a herd she was studying. A few weeks later, the elephant's family happened to pass through Moss's camp area. They walked in a long line, with the older elephants in front and the small babies between their legs. The younger elephants were in the back. In all likelihood, the elephants were drawn to the jawbone by their sense of smell. Elephants do not have great vision; they almost certainly did not see it. But they have a very good sense of smell, and perhaps were able to smell the jawbone as they passed near the camp. They stood around it for what seemed like a long time, examining it, touching it, just being near it. Then they moved on. Long after the others had gone, one little seven-year-old elephant stayed behind. He touched the jawbone, turning it over with his feet. He lifted it up with his

little trunk and seemed just to stare at it. Then he delicately ran the tip of his trunk over the entire bone. It was as if he recognized it. Only very reluctantly did he put the bone down and hurry along to catch up with his troop.

Cynthia Moss became curious and checked her records. Sure enough, the dead elephant had had a seven-year-old son. She concluded that this seven-year-old must have been the son and that somehow he had recognized his mother. Perhaps he recognized her by smell or by touch. When elephants greet each other, they intertwine trunks, clicking tusks and running their trunks all over each other's head. By whatever senses and signs, he knew it was his mother. And we can speculate that recognizing her gave him a strong feeling.

Can we know what the feeling was? Was he sad? Did he miss his mother and feel separated from her? I would think so. Did he remember the days when she was alive? That is possible, too. But it is also possible that the young elephant felt some emotion that we humans do not even know or recognize, some elephantine mixture of love, sadness, and memory particular only to elephants. It is humbling to think that animals, in particular elephants, who live in such complex social groups, may well have emotions that humans cannot even imagine. Or rather, we can imagine them, but we cannot get much closer than that. What we can know for certain is that we are not the only creatures on earth with deep feelings. The forests and jungles, and maybe even our own backyards, are full of animals who feel as profoundly as we do.

CHAPTER FOURTEEN

Four SHORT STORIES about DOGS

ou have all heard remarkable stories of dogs who, when lost, find their way home across vast distances. I have always wondered just how true those stories are. How could such a story be proved? An English veterinary surgeon tells of a case that he was able to authenticate. Dinah, a pregnant red setter, was sent by train to a town in England twenty-five miles away from her home. Shortly after she arrived, she gave birth to five puppies. The next day she disappeared, and the puppies disappeared with her. Ten days later she was found in her old home, in her favorite spot, asleep with all her puppies nestled close to her. Her feet were raw and bleeding, however, and she was terribly skinny. Obviously she had found her way home on foot—and brought her puppies with her. She must have carried each puppy one at a time, in relays of short distances. She would carry one, then go back and get the second puppy, then the third, fourth, and fifth. And then she would do that all over again, for another short segment of the trip home. Overall, she probably traveled ten times twenty-five miles! On her way, she had to cross the deep Blackwater River, eighty yards wide. Again, she must have done it one puppy at a time, swimming with each one in her mouth, leaving the rest on the shore to wait for her return. Her owners were so amazed at her deed that of course they kept her. Dinah proved herself a wonderful mom.

W HEN I WAS IN FRANCE, I heard a story that disturbed me a great deal. A man decided to get rid of a dog who had lived with him for many years. He put his dog into a boat and rowed out to the middle of the Seine River in Paris. Then he lifted up the dog and threw him overboard. The poor dog swam back to the boat and tried to climb aboard, but the man pushed him back into the water again. Once more the bewildered dog swam to the boat and tried to get in. This time, in attempting to push the dog back into the water, the man himself accidentally fell into the water. Unable to swim, he began to cry out for help. But it was early in the morning, and there was nobody around to hear his cries. Nobody except his dog, that is. And the dog knew

what to do: he swam up to his heartless master, grabbed him by his shirt collar, and swam with him back to shore. The dog saved the man's life. I do not know what happened to the dog or the man: I would like to think that the man learned his lesson and was never cruel to the dog again.

NOT LONG AGO A WOMAN was walking on a path overlooking the Oregon coast. She was not alone: she was walking with her old, blind golden retriever. Suddenly she heard a voice crying out: "Help! Help! I am drowning!" A fifteen-year-old girl had swum out too far into the ocean and was being carried away by the current. To the woman's surprise, her old golden immediately ran down the embankment in the direction of the calls and paddled out into the ocean. She reached the girl and, grabbing her bathing suit in her mouth, started to swim. People on the shore, who did not know the dog was blind, noticed that the dog seemed to be swimming in circles. When they began shouting to her, she was able to orient herself to their voices and head straight for the shore. Can you imagine how proud her owner was, and what a hero's welcome this blind old dog received!

A PROFESSOR AT TOKYO UNIVERSITY in Japan had a dog called Hachi-Ko. The professor had lived with the dog ever since he was a tiny puppy. They were very close, so close that it was agony for the dog to be separated from the professor. But since the professor left home every day to teach at the university, the dog had to be alone. So eager was Hachi-Ko to be with his friend that every single day, in the late afternoon, he would trot off to the Shibuya railroad station, about one mile from where the professor lived, and wait patiently for the train carrying the professor to arrive. When the professor's train arrived at six o'clock, Hachi-Ko was always there. Then he would carry out his duty of helping the professor find his way home. He would trot in front of him, looking very proud as the dignified professor walked behind, a little bit lost in his own thoughts.

One bitterly cold day in 1925, Hachi-Ko came at the usual time to the train station. But when the train arrived, the professor did not get off. How could Hachi-Ko know that the professor had died at work and would never take the train again? Some friends of the professor found the little dog still waiting at the train tracks the next day. They realized what had happened and took the dog home with them. The next day, however, Hachi-Ko left the new house in time to be at the train station for the arrival of the six o'clock train. This time, when his beloved friend did not come, he returned to his new home. Hachi-Ko went to the train station the next day, and the day after that, and every day for the next week, for the next month, in fact, for ten whole years—the rest of his life. He waited for the professor who never arrived. People came from near and far to see him, but he paid no attention. He was completely absorbed in waiting. So many people knew about Hachi-Ko and his great loyalty that when he died at the age of twelve, a day of national mourning was declared.

What do you think these four stories, all true, tell us about dogs?

CHAPTER FIFTEEN

ANIMALS and a SENSE of BEAUTY

ave you ever walked up a hill to watch the sun set? Did you ever take a friend with you? If so, you might have held his or her hand as you walked. If you were doing this in Africa in Gombe National Park, imagine your surprise if, as you started your climb, you noticed two figures in the distance. They, too, were walking up the hill, and they, too, were holding hands. But as you got closer, you saw that these were not human figures, but two chimpanzees! And imagine how much more surprised you and your friend would be if, when you arrived at the top of the hill to watch the sun go down over Lake Tanganyika, you glanced around, and not far from you the two chimpanzees

had sat down and were also watching the spectacular play of color in the sky. And when the sun had set, why, they got up, just as you did, and headed down the hill!

This really did happen. Geza Teleki, a graduate student in primatology (the study of primates, primarily apes and monkeys), saw it and recorded it in his notebook. He could hardly believe his eyes, but it was true nonetheless. Other researchers had reported similar things. The primatologist Adriaan Kortlandt watched as a wild chimpanzee gazed at a particularly spectacular sunset for fifteen minutes, until darkness fell.

What were you doing when you watched the sun set? Why were you there? You were there because it was beautiful. To watch the sky change colors, the clouds becoming pink and then gold, to feel the day become quiet as even the birds stop chirping, and finally to see the glowing mound of reddish golden light sink behind the horizon—who is not filled with strange feelings beholding all this? You watch the sun set because you have a sense of beauty.

Well, evidently so do the chimpanzees. Can we admit that chimpanzees and other animals enjoy beautiful sights just as we do? People who observe bears in the wild say that sometimes they see bears, too, sitting on top of a hill watching the sun set.

How many other animals have a sense of beauty? The lovely, unusual bowerbirds of New Guinea build very beautiful nests, called bowers. They put little bits of colored objects in them: flowers, fruits, insect parts, and other shining items. They even paint parts of the bower with charcoal and crushed berries, using a bark brush! Sometimes they visit one another's bowers and steal decorations. Some bowerbirds seem to prefer a certain color. The satin bowerbird—a blue-eyed species—likes blue items, for example. We humans find these bowers beautiful. But it would seem that the nests are beautiful not only to us. Male birds build their nests to impress the females, and the females indeed seem impressed, for they will often choose to mate with the birds who have built the most beautiful nests, in our opinion and seemingly in theirs.

D O ANIMALS LIKE TO listen to music? It is hard to believe that the songs of birds exist for reasons that have nothing to do with their beauty. I think birds like to sing, that they find pleasure, even joy, in doing it, and that they like to listen to the sounds. But do birds of one species enjoy the music of another species? Do they always prefer their own sounds, or are they like certain musicians who travel to another country and come to prefer that music to their own?

Researchers studying elephants in Kenya make their camp in the middle of the East African bush. Sometimes at night the people sing and play guitars, and the elephants draw near

to listen. Perhaps the elephants are merely curious about the human beings, but perhaps, too, they take pleasure in the music. Many humans love to listen to the underwater sounds that whales make. And some musicians have sat in small boats out in the ocean, playing to groups of whales. Sometimes the whales will just float beside them, their eyes closed, apparently listening in pleasure to the sound of a human flute.

M Y CONCLUSION IS THAT animals feel many of the same things that we do. They love their children. They form friendships and feel emotions of closeness and intimacy with other animals. They can miss their parents or companions and feel sad and nostalgic. They can feel compassion, even for a member of another species, and want to help even if they put their own safety at risk. They take delight in the physical world. They feel love and joy, terror and fear.

Animals may also have access to some emotions that we do not. For dogs—and elephants, too—smell is so important that it may introduce them to a whole universe of feelings unknown to us. It is hard to imagine the feeling world of a spider or a snake or an ant, yet I am convinced they have their own feelings, too, probably very different from anything we have ever felt.

Some animals may experience the same feelings we do—perhaps more intensely. People who do painful experiments on animals such as rabbits, for instance, claim that the rabbits do not feel pain, at least not the way humans do. One important difference, they say, is that humans can speak about their suffering. We can tell somebody what we are feeling. But I think it is wrong to say that because rabbits—or any animal—cannot use human language, they cannot suffer. The truth might be exactly the opposite. Precisely because animals cannot talk about their pain in language, they may feel it all the more acutely. Consider what happens when a child is in pain: he tells his mother. His mother can then explain something about it: how long it will last, what it comes from. She can comfort him with words, assuring him that the pain will go away and that soon he will feel better. When a child is too young to be comforted by words, the sensations of pain may be overwhelming. That child is in the same situation as an animal. Neither can be comforted through language. Nor would it be right to do so. A person experimenting on a rabbit could tell the rabbit only that the pain will soon be over by promising a quick death. If the rabbit could understand, that would be small consolation.

People have also claimed, rightly or wrongly, that animals have no sense of time. If true, then that is still another reason why their suffering must be more intense than ours. They cannot know that their pain will end soon, or ever. For an animal who lives only in the moment, the suffering must feel eternal. There is no prospect of a speedy end to the suffering, only endless pain. Moreover, the reason that people use certain animals for experiments is often because they know that that kind of animal is sensitive in a specific organ. Rabbits, for example, have very sensitive eyes. So some researchers in the cosmetic industry force their eyes open and pour stinging chemicals into them. This may well tell us something about what chemicals might be dangerous for human use, but at what a tremendous cost! Do most of us want to use chemicals or products that have caused animals great suffering? Does this poor planet really need another kind of floor polish, one of the many products tested on animals? Does it need to blind thousands of rabbits for yet one more shampoo?

If animals experience more or less the same emotions that we do, some we do not, and some more intensely than we do, does this mean that we have certain obligations to them? Yes, it does, in my opinion. I do not think we should eat them. Even if animals do eat other animals, we have the enormous privilege of choosing what we eat. We are practically the only animal that has that luxury. Nor does it seem to me a very good argument for eating meat to say that animals eat other animals. A male lion who takes over a pride may kill the cubs who are not his. Does this mean that human fathers should do the same? I do not think we should experiment on animals. I do not think we should wear their skins or fur. I do not think we should hurt them in any way whatsoever. They are our brothers and sisters, or at least our cousins. We are linked together, for the earth upon which we all walk and upon which we all depend is in trouble now.

We must try to bring it out of trouble, to restore some of the balance that existed before we came along and began doing things to upset it. If we stop harming the creatures on the earth, our animal cousins, then maybe we will also learn not to harm the trees, flowers, forests, and mountains. We will then surely treat one another with more loving-kindness as well. Perhaps we will come to see even rocks as our friends, as companions, objects of power and beauty. That day is probably a long way off for most people. But maybe for you and some of your friends, and for me, it is just around the corner. Maybe all we need to do is decide that we will become friends with animals, and trees, and rocks, and do them no harm, ever again, to the very best of our abilities.

❖

SOURCE NOTES

ABOUT THE AUTHOR
& ILLUSTRATOR

INDEX

❖

❖ SOURCE NOTES ❖

CHAPTER ONE ❖ The story about the elephant who saves the rhinoceros comes from Ralph Helfer, in his book *Beauty of the Beasts*, Los Angeles: Jeremy P. Tarcher, 1990, pp. 109–10.

CHAPTER TWO ❖ The source for the story about Ma Shwe comes from J. H. Williams's book, *Elephant Bill*, Garden City, New York: Doubleday, 1950, pp. 82–84.

CHAPTER THREE ❖ The story of the mother cat is from the book by Jane Martin and J. C. Suarès, *Scarlett Saves Her Family*, New York: Simon & Schuster, 1997.

CHAPTER FOUR ❖ The episode of Binti-Jua saving the three-year-old boy was widely reported in the world press in August 1996. See Frans B. M. de Waal, "Survival of the Kindest: A Simian Samaritan Shows Nature's True Heart," *The New York Times*, August 22, 1996, A2.

CHAPTER FIVE ❖ The story of the grizzly bear and the kitten was widely reported in the American press in 1996. See, for example, *People*, March 18, 1996, p. 62. I visited Wildlife Images in Grants Pass, Oregon, and spoke with the son of the founder, Dave Sidon, who showed me the bear and gave me more details about the incident.

CHAPTER SIX ❖ The stories of friendships between dogs and other animals are taken from my book *Dogs Never Lie About Love: Reflections on the Emotional World of Dogs*, New York: Crown Books, 1997; and from stories told to me by people after having read my book.

CHAPTER SEVEN ❖ The story of Freddie the Fly comes from the book by J. Allen Boone, *Kinship with All Life*, New York: Harper & Row, 1954.

CHAPTER EIGHT ✤ Obviously I alone am the (sadder but wiser) source of this story!

CHAPTER NINE ✤ The story of the African gray parrot, Alex, is told in *When Elephants Weep: The Emotional Lives of Animals* by Jeffrey Moussaieff Masson and Susan McCarthy, New York: Delacorte, 1995, pp. 19–20; it comes from interviews with Dr. Irene Pepperberg in 1993.

CHAPTER TEN ✤ The story about the elephant who was adopted comes from a film by Derek and Beverly Joubert, *Reflections on Elephants*: National Geographic Society.

CHAPTER ELEVEN ✤ Sheila Siddle, the director of the Chimfunshi Wildlife Orphanage Trust in Chingola, Zambia, sent me this video. It was reported in the *BBC Wildlife Magazine* for May 1996, p. 98.

CHAPTER TWELVE ✤ The story of the peregrine falcons comes from the book by Marcy Cottrell Houle, *Wings for My Flight*, Reading, Mass.: Addison-Wesley, 1991, pp. 75–87.

CHAPTER THIRTEEN ✤ The story about the baby elephant recognizing his mother from her bones is from Cynthia Moss's book, *Elephant Memories*, New York: William Morrow, 1988, pp. 272–73.

CHAPTER FOURTEEN ✤ These stories come from different sources. I have talked about them in my book *Dogs Never Lie About Love*, op. cit.

CHAPTER FIFTEEN ✤ The sense of beauty in animals comes from stories told by me in *When Elephants Weep: The Emotional Lives of Animals*, op. cit.

JEFFREY MOUSSAIEFF MASSON is the author of several national best-sellers, including *When Elephants Weep: The Emotional Lives of Animals* and *Dogs Never Lie About Love*. As a youth, he was the sole vegetarian and antihunting activist at his school in Hollywood, California. He is glad to live in a world now where more and more young people are able to express their love for animals in ways that were not possible when he was growing up.

"As we grow older," Mr. Masson says, "we lose some of the depth of those early feelings that children and animals retain."

Mr. Masson has a Ph.D. in Sanskrit from Harvard University and graduated from the Toronto Psychoanalytic Institute. He lives in Berkeley, California, with his wife and child and says he looks forward to moving his family to the country where they can have lots and lots of animals.

SHIRLEY FELTS grew up in southern Texas, surrounded by animals—cats, chickens, rabbits, dogs, a horse, and a cow. It was there that she developed a love of nature and started sketching plants, trees, and wildlife.

Ms. Felts graduated from the University of Texas with a degree in fine art, and since then has had many exhibitions of her paintings and has illustrated numerous books. Posters and prints of her work are sold around the world. In 1996 and in 1997, the Iwokrama International Rain Forest Research Program invited her to work from their field station, based on the south bank of the mighty Essequibo River in Guyana.

Ms. Felts lives in London with her husband, a landscape architect, and their black cat, Olive. They have two grown sons and a daughter.